MONSTAR'S
Perfect Pet

There are lots of Early Reader
stories you might enjoy.

Look at the back of the book or,
for a complete list, visit
www.orionchildrensbooks.co.uk

MONSTAR'S
Perfect Pet

STEVE COLE
Illustrated by PETE WILLIAMSON

Orion
Children's Books

ORION CHILDREN'S BOOKS

First published in Great Britain in 2016 by Hodder and Stoughton

1 3 5 7 9 10 8 6 4 2

Text copyright © Steve Cole, 2016
Illustrations copyright © Pete Williamson, 2016

The moral rights of the author and illustrator have been asserted.

A CIP catalogue record for this book
is available from the British Library.

ISBN 978 1 4440 1463 1

Printed and bound in China

The paper and board used in this book are from well-managed forests
and other responsible sources.

Orion Children's Books
An imprint of
Hachette Children's Group
Part of Hodder and Stoughton
Carmelite House
50 Victoria Embankment
London EC4Y 0DZ

An Hachette UK Company

www.hachette.co.uk
www.hachettechildrens.co.uk

For Amy, whose idea it was

Contents

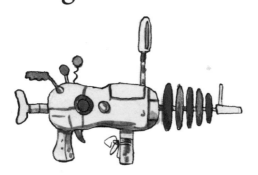

Chapter One

Monstar was Jen and Jon's green and fluffy pet.

She was a monster with a star over one eye.
That's why they called her Monstar.

Monstar loved to play in the big park.
She rode on the roundabout.

She played on
the swings.

She helped
the children
with their
games.

Monstar saw other people in the big park, walking their pets.

Big pets.

Small pets.

Unusual pets.

Monstar thought about pets all the way home.
"Me want a pet!" she said.

Chapter Two

"A pet for Monstar!" said Jon.
"What a lovely idea!" said Jen.
"Let's ask Mum and Dad."

Mum and Dad were inventing
something in the kitchen.
"It's a size ray," Mum said. "It can
make small things big and big
things small."

"Clever." Monstar licked Dad's ear.
"Please can me have a pet?"
"Hmmm." Dad pointed the size
ray at a ladybird.

"How about this?"
He switched on the ray.

ZAP!
The ladybird grew VERY big!

Chapter Three

Monstar gasped. "Me not want giant ladybird pet!"
Dad zapped it back to normal.
Mum patted Monstar. "I know just the pet for you."

Jen and Jon went with Mum and Monstar to a house in the next street.

That was when Monstar met...

HAMSTAR!

"He's a hamster with a star over one eye," said Mum's friend. "He's looking for a good home."

Jen clapped her hands. "That's perfect!"

Monstar picked him up. "Me
LOVE him!"
Hamstar ran up Monstar's furry
arm and climbed onto her head.
He looked very happy.

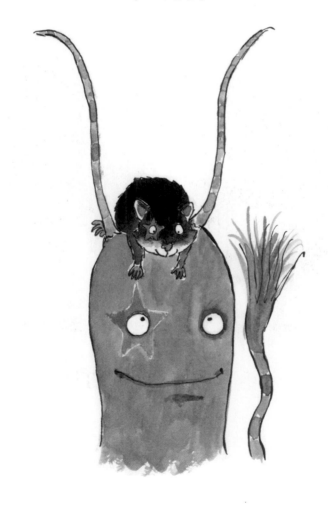

"All right. Hamstar can come to live with us." Mum wagged a finger. "But you must take good care of him. Promise?"

"Promise," said Monstar.
Jen and Jon nodded too.

"All right, then." Mum grinned.
"I'll build him a nice big cage as
soon as we get him home!"

Chapter Four

Hamstar had the best cage ever.

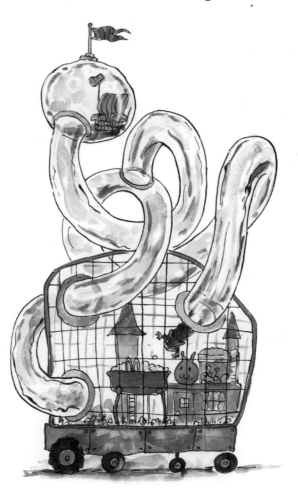

He had the best hamster ball.
He had the happiest owner too!

Monstar played with Hamstar
every day.
    She cleaned out his cage.
        Changed his water.
            Fed him food.

And made him his very own tutu!

But the tutu was too small.
"Oh, no!" Monstar groaned. "Now
what me do?"

Then she remembered the size ray.
It was still in the kitchen.

If she made the tutu a teeny bit bigger… it would fit Hamstar!

She put the tutu on the table and switched on the size ray. ZAP! The ray glowed green.

Hamstar jumped in front of it!

Chapter Five

Monstar gasped. Hamstar and the tutu were getting bigger…

BIGGER…

BIGGER!

Monstar couldn't find the
off-switch. "Help!" she cried.

Jen and Jon ran into the kitchen.
They yelled at the sight of the
giant Hamstar.

Hamstar was scared. BOOM!
He smashed through the kitchen
wall and ran away!

"Quickly," said Jen, grabbing the size ray. "Follow that Hamstar!" The giant Hamstar squashed Mum's garden shed. He flattened Dad's car. He knocked over a tree.

"I can't watch!" Jon covered his eyes. "What are we going to do?"
Monstar blinked.
Now, she had an idea!

Chapter Six

Monstar ran back to the kitchen and picked up Hamstar's tutu. The size ray had made it very, very big.

Mum came in and saw the hole in the wall. Her hair stood on end! "What is going on?"

"Er… Hamstar playing hide and seek," said Monstar. "Me seeking!" Taking the tutu, she ran off.

At first Monstar couldn't find her pet. But she could see people running away. She could hear people shouting.

Monstar followed the noise… and
gasped.

There was Hamstar, stomping
along the High Street!

Jen and Jon were trying to point the size ray at Hamstar. It was no good. He was too fast.

"Hamstar's heading for the park," said Jon. "There's lots for him to nibble there."

"Me got idea," said Monstar.
"Me must get there before him!"
Jen and Jon stared as Monstar
raced past her pet and vanished
from sight.

"Whatever is she up to?" said Jen.

Chapter Seven

As soon as she reached the park, Monstar dropped the giant tutu.

She got busy digging a hole
in the grass.

A very big hole.
A very, VERY big hole.

Hamstar's giant nose twitched as he entered the park. Jen and Jon came puffing up behind him with the size ray.

"Here, boy!" Monstar jumped and waved.
        "Over here!"

Hamstar didn't notice the hole in front of him.
PLOP. He fell into it!

As his huge, hairy head popped up, Monstar threw the giant tutu over him.

It covered his eyes so he couldn't see!
And because he couldn't see, he couldn't run away again.

"Good work, Monstar!" cried Jon, as Jen switched on the size ray. ZAP!

Hamstar shrank back down to normal size.

Monstar hopped into the hole and
scooped him up. "Me got you!"
She held him close. "Perfect size
for hugs again!"

Chapter Eight

Mum and Dad were NOT happy with the hole in their wall. But they were pleased that Hamstar was safe and sound.

He was soon back in his cage with
a tasty carrot as if nothing had
happened.

Luckily, Mum and Dad's amazing
inventions fixed the damage
Hamstar had done.

And Monstar covered up the hole
in the wall – with the giant tutu!
"Much prettier," she said.

When the wall was fixed, Monstar kept that tutu with her special things.

It was a souvenir of the day she saved her perfect pet.